The Noble Slut

Reclaiming Male Sexuality with Integrity, Freedom, and Connection

Ethan Jax Wilde

The Noble Slut

Copyright © 2025 by Ethan Jax Wilde

E BOOK: 978-1-968165-65-9

PAPERBACK: 978-1-968165-66-6

HARDBACK: 978-1-968165-67-3

Published by **Author Publications**: 2025

https://www.authorpublications.com

+1 (771) 203-5560

Printed in the United States of America

Dedication

To the wild, the misunderstood, and those with the courage it takes to live a life on your own terms. This is for the soul that refuses to be tamed and finds beauty in its own unique truth.

Acknowledgment

First and foremost, I am grateful for the unwavering love and patience of my family and friends. Your belief in me and this project gave me the space to create this book. I never would have thought my "Jerry Maguire" moment of brutal introspective honesty and conscientious epiphany, would turn into this amazing project. Thank you again to my family and friends who have encouraged and supported me in this endeavor, you know who you are.

My deepest gratitude also goes to my publishing team at Author's Publisher for their sharp insight and encouragement, and for believing in this project from the very beginning. To the early readers and critics, your honest feedback was and still is invaluable.

This book is a testament to the idea that our experiences create our stories, our stories are our power, and I couldn't have told mine and dedicated my life to living authentically without you.

About the Author

Ethan Jax Wilde has lived a life defined by discipline, introspection, and second chances. Shaped by decades of diverse experiences, he has navigated the complexities of relationships and the profound journey of masculine growth and fatherhood. His unique worldview comes from a life rich with lessons learned, even from the most well-intentioned missteps.

After a long road of self-discovery and reinvention, he found peace by embracing what he could not change and gathering the courage to change what he could. Ethan Jax Wilde is now committed to living a life of unapologetic authenticity, integrity, and respect alongside his wonderful partner with the desire to create an amazing future full of unimaginable memories and a legacy of a life well lived, even if it took a few broken Texas roads.

Foreword

I spent years trying to fit myself into the rigid confines of monogamy and, later, into a form of ethical nonmonogamy that still felt inauthentic. I'd punish myself for what I felt and desired, until I finally realized that true happiness lay in unapologetic self-acceptance. This was more than just physical freedom; it was about embracing the full, messy truth of who I am.

A crucial part of this awakening came from a book I read and reread: **"The Ethical Slut"** by Dossie Easton and Janet Hardy. Their work, though aimed at women, gave me the tools to unlock a new way of thinking about my own sexuality.

My 25 years in this "lifestyle" have been a mix of incredible adventures and painful misadventures. I've had loads of fun, but I've also made many mistakes, caused hurt feelings, and damaged relationships. After decades of this, I began to ask myself tough questions about what makes a relationship truly honorable.

This book is my answer. It's a guide to help men become the sexual, authentic individuals they are meant to be—but to do it in a **noble** way. For too long, men have used manipulation and deception to get what they want. We have lost the art of chivalry, self-respect, and integrity.

My hope is that the ideas in this book will help you regain your sense of sexual masculinity and honor. I hope they will help you not only become a better man in your relationships but a better man, period.

Let's regain our nobility.

Table of Contents

Chapter 1
Reclaiming Male Sexuality Without Shame

Finding Your Authentic Path

Remember the feeling? The primal urge, swiftly followed by a chilling wave of shame or confusion. This has been the unspoken story of male sexuality for far too many and far too long. We were led by conflicting messages. We are to be sexual conquerors, but don't catch feelings; desire constantly but never talk about it honestly. This internal contradiction has left generations of men feeling lost, repressed, and disconnected from their authentic selves.

The Blueprint of Bygone Eras: From "Stud" to Suppressed

For generations, particularly Gen X, the blueprint for male sexuality was clear: be a "stud," not a "slut." This wasn't about liberation; it was about performance. Movies, music, and even family conversations reinforced the idea that a man who "got around" was cool, masculine, and successful. Emotional detachment was often celebrated as a sign of strength, while vulnerability was considered a weakness. Think James Bond or Han Solo—men who took what they wanted and never cried.

What was conspicuously absent from this narrative were crucial concepts like **consent, emotional intelligence, and sexual ethics**. The lesson was not about connection, but conquest.

This drive for "more notches on the belt" came at a steep cost. How many men have walked away from casual encounters feeling emptier than before? Or found themselves trapped in a cycle of short-lived flings, wondering why true connection felt so out of reach? We were rewarded for being emotionally unavailable and penalized for being tender. This emotional repression isn't just a personal struggle; it contributes to societal issues like higher rates of depression and anxiety in men, and significant difficulty forming lasting, intimate bonds.

A Legacy of Mixed Messages: Generational Perspectives

Each generation of men has inherited a slightly different, yet consistently confusing, set of sexual rules.

Baby Boomers emerged from an era of repression into the free-love movement. The unspoken rule: have sex, but don't talk about feelings. They were conditioned to view sex as a purely physical act, often struggling to connect deeply with a spouse and seeking validation elsewhere.

Gen X grew up under the shadow of AIDS and hyper-sexualized media. They were told sex was dangerous, yet simultaneously that it was the ultimate measure of their masculinity. Raised on a diet of raunchy comedies that glorified conquest, they learned disassociation: sex was action, not emotion. This is a direct impediment to exploring ethical non-monogamy, which demands radical honesty.

Millennials came of age with the digital revolution, where porn became instantly accessible. While more open-minded than previous generations, many were burdened by shame, anxiety, and unrealistic depictions of sex. They inherited the legacy of emotional avoidance, mixed with new pressures from the internet.

Gen Z is the first generation to grow up with more widespread language around consent and mental health. They are generally more open to therapy and questioning traditional norms. However, this awareness often comes with its own overwhelm: the pressure to "get it right" can lead to anxiety or a new form of disconnection masked as performative "wokeness."

Across all these generations, a common thread emerges as men have been flooded with sexual stimulation but starved for genuine guidance. We've been taught how to want, but rarely how to honor that wanting with dignity, respect, and emotional integrity.

Reclaiming What Was Ours All Along: The Noble Slut Archetype

Decades later, many men are waking up, realizing they want something different. Not less sex, but more realness. Not fewer partners, but more depth. Not domination, but connection.

We've been molded to believe our sexuality should conform to specific societal norms, leading to profound internal conflict. We struggle to reconcile these ideals with our true selves, often repressing, ignoring, and even hating who we are sexually. But when we gain emotional intelligence to explore and accept our sexuality, we find profound peace.

This self-acceptance is crucial; it can embolden those who struggle with sexual identity issues and ultimately aid in easing mental health burdens.

The truth is, your sexuality isn't something to be hidden, weaponized, or apologized for. It's a gift—and if treated with awareness, it can lead to deeper connection, more authentic relationships, and a peace most of us never knew was possible.

This journey isn't just about recovering our authentic desire; it's about embodying a new archetype: **The Noble Slut**. This isn't about promiscuity for its own sake, but about embracing sexual freedom not through conquest or deception, but through **integrity, enthusiastic consent, and genuine connection**. It's about being honest about what you want, honoring others' autonomy, and building relationships— monogamous or non-monogamous—on a foundation of mutual respect.

A New Path Forward

I've seen it firsthand: the world tells men to be sexual beasts and emotional rocks, but then it turns around and punishes you for being too much of either. It's a brutal, rigged game, a double standard that leaves you either ashamed of your own damn desires or so detached from your feelings you don't even know what's real anymore.

Forget the guides on how to "get more women" or achieve sexual mastery over others, those will leave you feeling alone and self-loathing, as well as have a reputation that would run off even the strongest of potential partners. This book is about getting real with yourself, understanding and accepting who you really are. It's about reconnecting with what you want, learning to stop hurting others (and yourself) along the way, and finally living your sexual life without shame or pretense.

Being a "slut" isn't the problem. Being a coward, a liar, or a manipulator is, and frankly, most men were never shown a different way. Male desire isn't evil; it's just been running blind. If you've ever felt stuck between wanting total freedom and wanting true intimacy or felt like you're a fraud even when you were trying to love, know this: YOU are not alone. You're not broken. You just haven't been given a map.

The Noble Slut is that map.

This book isn't here to challenge you to question everything; it's here to show you a better way. You're about to unlearn every lie you've been told about masculinity, sex, and relationships. It's about owning your desires without manipulating others, building relationships on honesty instead of pretense, and communicating like a man who respects himself and those he loves. This is your invitation to embrace your sexuality without guilt or shame.

Welcome to a new version of manhood—one that doesn't rely on monogamy or relationships for meaning, dominance for power, or silence for strength. You can be ethical. You can be open. You can be slutty. And you can be noble.

Let's begin.

Chapter 2
What Does It Mean to Be an Ethical Man?

Building Trust in Every Connection

Everyone knows that a guy who faked a business trip to be with someone else isn't just lying—he's a coward. That deception doesn't just hurt; it shatters trust and poisons any chance of a real connection. It's a classic example of how a lack of ethical grounding leads to total emotional wreckage. Being "ethical" isn't about being perfect or following a rigid set of rules. It's a daily commitment to show up with honesty, enthusiastic consent, and a genuine goddamn care for the people you're with. It's a test of integrity in every intimate interaction. It's not a destination—it's just the work.

Being "ethical" isn't about being perfect or following a rigid set of rules. It's about a continuous practice of showing up honestly, with enthusiastic consent, and genuine care and consideration. It's a commitment to integrity in all your interactions, especially those that are intimate. It's a journey, not a destination.

The Ethics of Honesty and Integrity

An ethical man doesn't lie to get laid. He doesn't gaslight or manipulate. He doesn't promise monogamy if he genuinely doesn't want it. Crucially, he doesn't use the language of "freedom" to dodge emotional responsibility or avoid difficult conversations. These aren't just "bad behaviors"; they are antithetical to the very authentic connection he claims to seek. True freedom in relationships comes from trust and clarity, not from evasion.

An ethical man doesn't lie to get what he wants. He doesn't gaslight or manipulate, and he doesn't promise monogamy if he doesn't genuinely want it. He also doesn't use the language of "freedom" to dodge emotional responsibility or avoid difficult conversations. These aren't just mistakes; they're the opposite of the authentic connection he claims to seek. True freedom in relationships isn't the absence of responsibility; it's the acceptance of it.

If you desire the freedom to explore multiple connections, then you must also accept the profound responsibility of being transparent, emotionally intelligent, and kind. This isn't just about avoiding harm; it's about actively building trust and fostering genuine, respectful connections, regardless of the number of partners involved. When you operate with integrity, you build a life that truly aligns with your values, free from the burden of secrecy and the gnawing anxiety of deception. This allows for deeper, more authentic connections because everyone involved knows they are being treated with respect and honesty.

The Rules Haven't Changed: Ethics Matter in All Relationships

You might think "ethics" sounds too formal or academic for something as intimate as sex and relationships. But the truth is, without a strong ethical foundation, nonmonogamy—or any relationship structure—quickly devolves into chaos, hurt, and mistrust. Unlike traditional monogamous structures, where certain expectations are often implicitly understood, ethical nonmonogamy demands **explicit communication** and a proactive, unwavering commitment to integrity.

Think of it as building your "trust battery." Each honest conversation, each boundary respected, each act of care builds charge. Conversely, deception, evasion, or manipulation drains it, leaving you isolated, anxious, and ultimately, alone.

The Pillars of an Ethical Man

A man with a code doesn't need a rulebook. He has a foundation built on universal truths that hold up in any relationship. Here are the pillars of a truly ethical man, and I challenge YOU to begin making the changes in your life to live by them.

Radical Honesty: This goes far beyond simply not lying; it's about proactively sharing your desires, intentions, and boundaries—even when it's uncomfortable. It means being honest with yourself first, then with your partners.

This includes:

Disclosing New Connections Early: You don't wait for emotions to get tangled. You lay your cards on the table. On a third date, if you feel a connection, you say: "I'm enjoying this, but I want to be upfront because I'm also seeing other people. How do you feel about that?" You give them a choice, with all the facts.

Being Honest About Evolving Feelings: Emotions are dynamic. Don't suppress them for convenience. For example, if a casual arrangement starts to feel more serious, be honest: "I initially thought this would be purely casual, but I'm finding myself developing deeper feelings for you. I wanted to be honest about that and see if this still aligns with what you're looking for."

Setting Clear Boundaries: Your needs and limits are non-negotiable. When you're overwhelmed and need space, you communicate that directly. Don't fall into the trap of becoming distant or irritable; speak your truth instead of shutting down.

Enthusiastic Consent: Beyond a simple "yes," enthusiastic consent means a clear, ongoing, conscious, and uncoerced agreement for every interaction, whether physical, emotional, or relational. It's about respecting boundaries, being highly attuned to your partner's comfort, and understanding that consent can be withdrawn at any time for any reason. This means learning your partner down to their core to understand he subtlest changes that can signal consent and even non-consent.

Checking In During Intimacy: Consent is not a one-time event. During sex, consistently ask: "Does this feel good? Is this pace okay for you?" And, crucially, "You can tell me if you want to stop at any point, and I'll respect that immediately." By being considerate of their feelings and desires, you are building a level of trust that builds a firm foundation.

Emotional Consent: Respect emotional space and readiness. Before sharing sensitive information about another partner, ask: "Is now a good time to talk about something personal, or would you prefer we wait?"

Consent for Public Disclosure: Before introducing partners to friends or posting about relationships on social media, obtain explicit consent from all involved.

Proactive Care and Empathy: An ethical man deeply considers the impact of his actions on others. This means being mindful of feelings, offering support, and being willing to engage in difficult, emotionally charged conversations. It's about ensuring all parties feel seen, heard, and valued.

Addressing Jealousy with Compassion: When a partner expresses jealousy, listen actively, validate their feelings, and explore solutions together. Don't dismiss it as "their problem."

Navigating Time Scarcity with Intentionality: If you have multiple partners or a demanding schedule, proactively ensure you're not neglecting anyone. "I know this week is busy, but I wanted to set aside time for us to connect because you're important to me."

Post-Encounter Check-Ins: After a new or intense experience, check in with a partner: "How are you feeling after our date last night? Was there anything that came up for you that you want to talk about?"

Clear Communication: This is the absolute bedrock upon which all other ethical principles stand. It's about expressing your needs, desires, and limits clearly and unambiguously. It also means actively listening to understand your partners, not just to respond.

Using "I" Statements: Take ownership of your feelings. Instead of saying, "You never tell me what you're feeling," try, "I feel disconnected when we don't talk about our emotions."

Setting Expectations for Relationship Style Upfront: From the very beginning of a new connection, be clear about what you're looking for.

Scheduling Regular Check-Ins: For complex dynamics, make difficult conversations less daunting by scheduling a regular time to talk about your week, needs, and feelings.

Taking Responsibility: Mistakes, better yet, screwups happen—and they will—an ethical man takes full ownership of his actions, apologizes sincerely, and actively works to repair any harm caused. It's about learning from missteps and demonstrating a genuine commitment to growth.

Owning a Communication Breakdown: If you screw up, acknowledge your part. "I realize I didn't communicate clearly about my schedule, and I truly apologize for that. Next time, I'll be more explicit."

Repairing a Breach of Trust: If you break confidence, take responsibility. "I messed up by sharing that private information. I completely understand if you feel betrayed. 'How can I begin to earn back your trust?"

Learning from Your Emotions: When jealousy gets the best of you, you own it. "My reaction was out of line. That was my jealousy talking, not you. I apologize, and I'm working on that."

The Journey of an Ethical Man

Being an ethical man in nonmonogamy isn't about achieving a static state of perfection. It's about a relentless, ongoing commitment to integrity, empathy, and personal growth. It's about deep understanding that the freedom to explore diverse connections comes with the profound responsibility to treat all involved with dignity, respect, and care.

This unwavering commitment protects you from the emotional wreckage of deception, secrets, and manipulation, allowing you to build a life rich in authentic, meaningful connections. It leads to deeper, more fulfilling relationships, significant personal growth, and a stronger, more integrated sense of self.

You'll find that living ethically isn't a burden; it's a liberation. It allows you to be truly **noble** in your "slutty" exploration of desire, cultivating relationships built on mutual respect and genuine care.

Chapter 3
Communicating Like a Man
(Who Gets It)

Most of us were never taught to say, "I feel scared" or "I need reassurance." Instead, we were conditioned to shut up, push through, or disappear. The prevailing masculine script dictated that vulnerability was weakness, and expressing emotion was a fast track to being seen as "less than." We learned to internalize our feelings, building walls instead of bridges, which inevitably led to misunderstandings, resentment, and profound isolation. It's almost as if society actively punished men for effective communication, making this journey toward emotional literacy an act of true courage.

In ethical relationships, communication isn't just important; it's the very foundation on which everything else depends."

If you desire the freedom that ethical non-monogamy or, in all actuality, any truly authentic relationship offers, you must pay for it in truth. This means becoming fluent in radical honesty, the art of saying what's real, even when it feels messy or uncomfortable. This isn't about being brutally frank; it's about courageous transparency rooted in deep respect for yourself and your partners.

You don't need to be a licensed therapist to communicate effectively. You need to be present. You need to listen to understand, not just to fix or wait for your turn to speak. You need to say what's true, not what's convenient. This chapter will equip you with the fundamental skills to navigate the nuanced landscape of ethical communication, ensuring your desires are honored, your needs are met, and your partners feel genuinely respected and seen.

The Myth of the Silent Strong Man

For generations, men were conditioned to believe that silence equated to strength. Our cultural heroes often grunted, nodded, and acted, rarely articulating their inner worlds. This archetype of the "strong, silent type" became a pervasive ideal, teaching us to suppress feelings and solve all problems alone. While stoicism might serve well in battle, it undermines intimacy, teaching us to suppress feelings and face problems alone, often at great cost to relationships.

Without open, honest, and consistent communication, assumptions fester, resentments build, and genuine emotional connection withers.

In non-monogamy, especially, the stakes of poor communication are incredibly high. What could be a liberating and deeply fulfilling experience quickly becomes a minefield of jealousy, confusion, and hurt. The success of any non-monogamous dynamic hinges almost entirely on the quality of communication among all involved.

Essential Communication Skills for the Noble Slut

Becoming a man who "gets it" means developing specific, actionable skills. These skills go beyond conflict resolution; they are about building deeper intimacy and fostering strong, lasting trust. Communication is much like a muscle—it grows only through consistent and intentional practice.

Think of communication as a muscle that requires consistent, intentional exercise to grow stronger.

1.   The Power of "I" Statements

This is foundational to non-blaming communication. Instead of accusing in a high stakes conversation, "I" statements focus on your own feelings and perceptions. This subtle shift puts the focus on your internal experience, which is something no one can genuinely argue with.

Don't say: "You always make me feel ignored when you spend time with her." (This is accusatory and implies intent.)

Do say: "I feel a bit insecure when you spend extended time with your new partner without checking in, because I need reassurance that our connection is still strong and a priority to me." (This expresses your feeling and the underlying need, allowing for a constructive conversation.) Here are some examples in both monogamous and ethically non-monogamous relationships.

Ethically Non-Monogamous: Chris and Dana

Do Say: Using "I" Statements

Dana: "Hey Chris, can we chat for a bit? I've been feeling a little disconnected from you lately. I've noticed that with the time you're spending with Jamie, I've started to feel like our connection is weakening, and that makes me feel a little insecure. I'd love for us to find a way to make sure we're still prioritizing our time together. Maybe we can schedule a consistent weekly date night or just check in with each other more often."

Why this works:

Focuses on feelings, not rules: Dana expresses their personal feelings ("I've been feeling a little disconnected") rather than accusing Chris of breaking a rule. This respects the open nature of their relationship.

Avoids assigning blame: The statement "I've noticed that with the time you're spending with Jamie, I've started to feel..." links the feeling to the situation without blaming Chris. It's about Dana's internal experience.

Proposes a solution: By suggesting a "consistent weekly date night" or "checking in more often," Dana actively seeks to restore their own sense of security and connection, making it a collaborative effort rather than a demand.

Don't Say: Using "You" Statements

Dana: "You're always with Jamie, and you're neglecting me. This whole non-monogamy thing is a mess. You're not being fair, and you're making me feel completely unimportant. You need to choose between me and them."

Why this doesn't work:

Attacks the partner and the relationship structure: The "YOU" statements are a direct attack on Chris ("You're always with Jamie") and the core agreement of their relationship ("This whole non-monogamy thing is a mess"). This will immediately trigger a defensive response.

Puts the partner in a difficult position: By saying, "You need to choose between me and them," Dana is introducing a condition that fundamentally goes against the principles of their agreement, which is ethically non-monogamous. It's a lose-lose situation for Chris.

Breaks down communication: The accusatory tone and ultimatum shut down any possibility of a productive conversation, forcing the issue into a conflict rather than a crucial conversation about needs and feelings.

Monogamous: Alex and Sam

Do Say: Using "I" Statements

Alex: "Hey Sam, can we talk for a minute? I've been feeling a little lonely and disconnected lately. When you're out late, I start to feel like I'm not a priority, and it makes me feel a little insecure. I'd love to find a way for us to connect more, maybe we could schedule a date night or just spend some more time together at home."

Why this works:

Focuses on feelings: Alex starts the conversation by sharing their own feelings ("I've been feeling a little lonely and disconnected"). This makes it about their experience, not about Sam's actions.

Avoids blame: There's no accusation. The statement "When you're out late, I start to feel..." links the feeling directly to the situation without saying, "You make me feel..."

Opens a dialogue: By expressing a need and suggesting a solution ("I'd love to find a way for us to connect more"), Alex invites Sam to be a partner in solving the issue rather than just defending themselves.

Don't Say: Using "You" Statements

Alex: "You're always going out with your friends and never make time for me. You're so selfish, and you make me feel like I don't matter to you at all. I don't even know why you're in this relationship."

Why this doesn't work:

Creates a defensive reaction: "YOU" statements often come across as accusations. Sam will likely feel attacked and immediately become defensive, leading to a shutdown or an argument.

Shifts blame: This statement places all the blame on Sam's behavior. Instead of expressing a personal feeling, it's a direct judgment of Sam's character ("You're so selfish").

Escalates the conflict: The conversation immediately becomes an attack, making it difficult to find a solution. It forces Sam to either accept the blame or fight back, neither of which leads to a productive outcome.

The Takeaway

The difference is clear. **"I" statements** allow you to express your feelings and needs without attacking your partner. They invite a productive conversation centered on mutual understanding and problem-solving. **"YOU" statements**, on the other hand, lead to blame, defensiveness, and conflict. The goal of a crucial conversation is to find a solution together, and "I" statements are the most effective tool to start that journey.

2. Active Listening: Beyond Just Hearing

Listening is more than waiting for your turn to respond. It requires an active, empathetic effort to truly understand your partner's perspective, emotions, and needs. It is not only about the words you speak but also about how you take in, process, and respond to what is being shared.

Reflect and summarize: Repeat back what you heard in your own words to confirm your understanding. For example: "So, if I'm understanding correctly, you're feeling overwhelmed by my date plans and need me to share less detail? Is that right?"

Validate feelings: Acknowledge and legitimize their emotion, even if you don't agree with their perspective. For example: "I can see why that would make you feel frustrated," or "It sounds like you're really hurting right now, and I'm sorry to hear that."

3. Proactive Check-ins: The Pulse of Your Relationships

Instead of waiting for a crisis, create regular opportunities to connect and address concerns before they build up. Consistent check-ins help prevent problems from escalating and ensure that everyone's changing needs are acknowledged. These moments serve as ongoing care for the relationship, not just emergency repairs.

Scheduled Check-ins: Agree on a regular time (e.g., weekly) to formally discuss how things are going. Discussion points could include: "How are you feeling about our relationship this week?" or "Is there anything you need more or less of from me right now?"

Spontaneous Check-ins: Briefly touch base when something feels off. For example: "Hey, I noticed you were a bit quiet after I mentioned my date plans for Saturday. Is everything okay?"

4. The Art of Negotiation and Compromise

Ethical communication isn't just about expressing your needs; it's about collaboratively finding solutions that work for everyone. This requires flexibility, creativity, and a genuine willingness to compromise.

Focus on shared solutions: Shift from an adversarial mindset ("It's my way or the highway") to a collaborative one. Ask: "How can we find a solution that addresses both our needs and feels good for everyone?"

Identify underlying needs: Often, surface-level conflicts are symptoms of deeper, unmet needs. For example: "It sounds like what you're really expressing is a need for more dedicated, uninterrupted quality time. How can we make that happen?"

5. Communicating Boundaries (Yours and Others')

You cannot expect partners to respect your boundaries if you haven't clearly and kindly articulated them. Likewise, you have a fundamental ethical obligation to actively listen for and respect their boundaries, even if you don't fully understand or agree with them. Boundaries are not about control; they are about self-respect and safety.

Clearly state your boundaries: Be explicit and direct. For example: "My boundary is that I need a full day's notice before any spontaneous dates with other partners, so I can mentally prepare."

Respect your partners' boundaries: When a partner states a boundary, acknowledge it immediately and adjust your behavior without argument or pushback. For example: "Okay, I understand you prefer not to hear explicit details about my sexual encounters with others. I'll make sure to keep those conversations focused on emotional connection and logistics instead."

The Payoff: Deeper Connections, More Freedom

Mastering communication—through honesty, listening, regular check-ins, negotiation, and clear boundaries—is one of the most important steps in building ethical relationships. Ethical communication means you create trust and intimacy without undermining your partners' needs. When practiced with consistency, it allows you to navigate complex situations with grace, strengthen authentic bonds, and live the freedom you seek in collaboration with others rather than at their expense.

What's one communication skill you're committed to practicing more consistently in your relationships, starting today?

Chapter 4
Jealousy, Fear, and Emotional Maturity
Navigating the Inner Landscape

Jealousy can and more than likely will exist to some degree in every type of relationship, especially in ethical non-monogamy. If you believe jealousy won't surface in ethical non-monogamy, you may be underestimating the reality of the experience or haven't yet fully stepped into it. Let's be unequivocally real: it's a powerful, often uncomfortable, but entirely human emotion.

Jealousy doesn't make you weak; it makes you human. What makes you strong is how you handle it. When your partner goes out with someone else, does your stomach drop? Do you feel a pang of panic? Good. That means you're alive and connected. The critical skill here is not to suppress those feelings—which only serve to make them stronger—but to sit with them, learn from them, and ultimately, grow through them.

These intense emotions are not roadblocks; they are vital signposts, pointing to deeper needs and fears within yourself.

This chapter provides you with practical tools for managing these emotional storms without trying to control others. That's the essence of emotional maturity—and its precisely how freedom works in practice.

The Illusion of Control

In traditionally monogamous relationships, there's often an unspoken agreement that your partner's attention and affection are exclusively yours. While this can offer security, it also fosters a false sense of control over another person's emotions. When you step into non-monogamy, this illusion is shattered. You are confronted with the reality that your partner is an autonomous individual with their own desires. This can trigger deep-seated fears of abandonment, inadequacy, or being replaced.

Unpacking Jealousy: More Than Just an Emotion

Jealousy is rarely a singular feeling. It's a complex cocktail of emotions. Understanding these components is the first step to dismantling this destructive power.

Fear: This is often the deepest root. It's fear of abandonment, fear of being replaced, or fear of not being "enough." If your partner comes home glowing from a date, your jealousy might stem from a subconscious fear that their joy with someone else means they'll eventually find you less appealing and leave.

Insecurity: This involves doubts about your own worth or desirability, often leading you to compare yourself unfavorably to your partner's new connections.

Envy: A longing for what your partner is experiencing. This is often less about the individual and more about the novelty, passion, or excitement of the experience itself.

Possessiveness: An unconscious belief that your partner or their attention "belongs" to you. This is a transactional view of relationships where a person is seen as an extension of oneself.

Loss of Control: The anxiety of not knowing or being able to direct your partner's every move, thought, or feeling.

Social Conditioning: The deeply ingrained belief, fueled by media and societal norms, that jealousy is a definitive "sign of true love."

The Monogamous Relationship and Jealousy:

Sarah and Mark have been in a monogamous relationship for three years. Mark is a marketing professional who recently started a new job. He's been spending a lot of time with his team, including a colleague named Emily, who is intelligent, funny, and outgoing. Sarah has never met Emily.

One evening, Mark tells Sarah about a successful project presentation he and Emily gave. He says, "Emily and I just clicked on this. We were a great team, and our boss was really impressed. She's hilarious, too."

The Feelings of Jealousy

When Sarah hears this, a wave of familiar, unpleasant feelings washes over her.

Fear: Sarah feels a pang of **fear** that Mark might be developing feelings for Emily. The thought of losing Mark, of being replaced, sends a shiver down her spine. The "click" he mentioned makes her heart beats faster.

Insecurity: The conversation triggers her **insecurity**. Sarah begins to compare herself to Emily. *Is Emily smarter than I am? More fun? Prettier?* She starts to question her own value and what she brings to the relationship, feeling she might not be "enough" for Mark.

Envy: Sarah feels **envy** towards Emily. She's envious of the time Emily gets to spend with Mark, the jokes they share, and the professional success they've achieved together. She wishes she were the one sharing those moments with him.

Possessiveness: A feeling of **possessiveness** creeps in. Sarah feels a sense of ownership over Mark's time and attention. She believes his emotional and social energy should be reserved primarily for her, especially if it's "getting close" with another woman.

Loss of Control: Sarah experiences a **loss of control**. She can't control who Mark works with, how they interact, or what he thinks. This lack of control over his environment and emotions makes her feel powerless and anxious.

The Role of Social Conditioning

These feelings aren't just a random reaction; they're heavily influenced by **social conditioning**.

The Monogamy Script: From fairy tales to romantic comedies, our culture reinforces the idea of "the one." This narrative dictates that a partner should fulfill all our emotional and social needs, and any significant connection with another person is a threat to the relationship. This script tells Sarah that Mark's connection with Emily is a direct danger to their bond.

Gender Roles: Traditional gender roles often portray men as "pursuers" and women as "gatekeepers" of relationships. This can make Sarah feel that she has to "guard" her man, and any female competition is a direct threat to her status as his partner.

The "Happily Ever After" Myth: Society presents a false reality where a committed relationship is free of external temptations or deep emotional connections with others. This myth leaves Sarah unprepared for the reality of adult relationships, where partners will inevitably form friendships and bonds outside of the primary couple. Her feelings of jealousy are reinforced by the notion that this shouldn't be happening in a "perfect" relationship.

The Non-Monogamous Relationship and Jealousy:

The Scenario

Chris and Dana are in a committed, ethically non-monogamous relationship. They have a shared understanding that they can both have other partners, as long as they practice **clear communication**, **honesty**, and **safe sex**. Chris has been dating a new partner, Alex, for a few months. Dana has met Alex and thinks she is a great person.

Lately, Chris and Alex have been spending more and more time together, to the point where they are beginning to share intimate jokes and talk about future travel plans. One night, Chris mentions that Alex is planning a surprise trip for them and that Alex even knows which specific tea they prefer.

The Feelings of Jealousy

When Dana hears this, her heart sinks. Even within their agreed-upon structure, these feelings bubble up.

Fear: Dana feels a sudden **fear** of being left behind. The idea of Chris and Alex having their own secret inside jokes and plans for the future makes Dana worry that their primary relationship with Chris is no longer the center of Chris's life.

Insecurity: Dana's **insecurity** is triggered by a feeling of being less "important" or "special." While Dana intellectually understands that Chris can love more than one person, the personalized gift and intimate knowledge of Chris's favorite tea make Dana question if they still hold a unique position in Chris's life.

Envy: Dana feels **envy** not just of Alex, but of the experiences Chris and Alex are sharing. Dana wishes they were the ones planning surprise trips and sharing inside jokes with Chris, creating a special world just for the two of them.

Possessiveness: A feeling of **possessiveness** emerges, a desire for Chris's emotional energy and time to be focused on Dana. Even with their open agreement, Dana feels a sense of ownership over Chris's intimate moments and feels a desire for Chris to seek their approval before making plans with another partner.

Loss of Control: Dana experiences a **loss of control**. Dana can't dictate the depth or speed of Chris's connection with Alex. This lack of control over the other relationship and the uncertainty it creates makes Dana feel anxious and powerless.

The Role of Social Conditioning

These feelings are intensified by deeply ingrained **social conditioning** around monogamy, even though they have chosen a different path.

The Monogamous Script in an Open World: Society's dominant narrative is that of a single, primary romantic partner who meets all your needs. When Dana sees Chris and Alex growing closer, this conditioning whispers, "This isn't how it's supposed to be. Something is wrong." It's hard to shake the idea that a "real" relationship is one where a partner's attention is focused solely on you.

The "One and Only" Myth: We are conditioned to believe in a singular love—a "soulmate." This myth creates a sense of competition for affection and importance. Even when you've agreed there isn't a "one and only," the myth makes it easy to feel like you're losing a competition when a partner gets closer to someone else.

Internalized Scarcity: Social conditioning teaches us that love is a finite resource. This belief creates a fear of having "less" love for yourself when a partner gives some to someone else. Even though ethically non-monogamous relationships are based on the idea of abundant love, this ingrained fear of scarcity is still there, making feelings of jealousy a real challenge to navigate.

These feelings, while they seem to contradict the values of an open relationship, are a normal part of "the human experience". The key is to communicate with your partner to find a way to work through them and not let them define the relationship.

Tools for Navigating Emotional Storms

Here's how an emotionally mature man approaches the inevitable waves of jealousy and fear:

Acknowledge and Feel (Don't Suppress): The goal isn't to not feel jealous, but to observe it without letting it dictate your actions.

Practice Self-Awareness: When jealousy hits, pause. Notice the physical sensations in your body (a tight chest, a racing heart). Identify the emotion as precisely as you can: "I'm feeling intense jealousy right now. And beneath that, I think I'm scared of being alone."

Give it a Name: Articulating the emotion—even just to yourself—helps to diffuse its intensity. You can journal it or mentally label it: "This is jealousy. This is fear of abandonment."

Allow the Feeling to Pass: Emotions are like waves. Don't fight them; observe them, acknowledge their presence, and allow them to move through you. This might involve deep breathing, taking a walk, or listening to music.

Self-Soothing and Regulation: Before addressing the situation outwardly, first learn to regulate your own emotional state. You can't have a productive conversation when you're in the throes of an emotional surge.

Grounding Techniques: Bring yourself back to the present moment. Name 5 things you can see, 4 things you can hear, 3 things you can feel, 2 things you can smell, and 1 thing you can taste.

Healthy Distraction: Engage in an activity you genuinely enjoy that fully absorbs your attention, like intense exercise or a creative hobby. This is not avoidance; it's a strategic temporary redirect.

Proactive Self-Care: A depleted emotional battery makes you more susceptible to intense negative emotions. Prioritize eating well, getting enough sleep, and regular exercise.

Curiosity Over Blame: Identifying the Root Cause Once you've regulated your initial emotional surge, approach the feeling with curiosity rather than judgment. What is this emotion really trying to tell you?

Ask "Why?": Delve deeper. "Why am I feeling this right now? Is it because I'm not getting enough attention? Is it a fear of being compared?"

Look Inward: Often, jealousy is about your own unmet needs or past wounds being triggered. Are you relying too heavily on your partner for all your validation?

Keep a Jealousy Journal: Track specific jealousy incidents. Note the trigger, your feelings, and what you think were the underlying fears or insecurities. This helps you identify recurring patterns and develop personalized coping strategies.

Communicate Your Needs (Not Your Demands) Once you understand what's truly driving your jealousy, you can communicate your needs to your partner in a constructive, non-accusatory way, utilizing the "I" statements discussed in Chapter 3.

Don't say: "You need to stop seeing [other person] because it makes me uncomfortable. You're making me feel bad." (This is a controlling demand that shifts blame.)

Do say: "When you spend multiple nights a week with your new partner, I feel a deep sense of loneliness and a fear of losing our unique connection. I need more reassurance about the stability of our relationship. Would you be open to having a dedicated date night each week, just for us?" (This expresses your feelings, identifies your need, and offers a collaborative solution.)

Compersion: The Counter-Emotion (Optional, But Powerful)

While not everyone experiences it, compersion is often described as the opposite of jealousy: the genuine, empathetic joy you feel when your partner is happy and fulfilled with someone else.

Focus on Your Partner's Happiness: Shift your focus from your own potential loss to your partner's gain. See their joy as a win for them, and indirectly, a win for your relationship.

Celebrate Their Experiences: Actively engage in their excitement. Ask them about their dates and genuinely share in their good feelings.

Connect Your Own Growth: Recognize that your partner's new connections often push you to grow individually, too—to explore new hobbies or deepen other friendships.

Emotional Maturity: The Foundation of Freedom

Managing jealousy and fear isn't about shutting down emotions. It's about mastering your inner world—observing, understanding, and skillfully navigating your feelings with clarity and self-awareness.

This discipline allows you to consistently choose connection over control, and to build relationships founded on genuine trust and mutual respect. The ethical man understands that true freedom in relationships isn't the absence of difficult feelings, but the capacity to navigate them with grace, integrity, and a profound commitment to his own growth and the well-being of those he loves.

Remember, you don't have to do this alone. It's courageous to seek support from a trusted friend, a relationship coach, or a therapist specializing in non-monogamy and emotional intelligence to help process these intense emotions.

Chapter 5
Sex, Pleasure, and Exploration: The Noble Lover's Path

When was the last time you truly felt present during sex, rather than being consumed by what you "should" be doing or achieving? For many men, the answer is "rarely," if ever.

We've been taught a script that prioritizes performance over genuine connection, leaving us feeling detached even in our most intimate moments.

The truth is, the best lovers aren't the ones who know every trick in the book; they're the ones who listen intently, respond authentically, and remain fully present with their partner. Ethical sex isn't about the number of partners or the intensity of the orgasm. It's about the quality of the experience, the unwavering respect for consent, the pursuit of mutual joy, and, perhaps most importantly, the profound absence of shame.

Do you want to explore kink, threesomes, or casual sex with genuine depth and integrity? Fantastic. But let it be an act of conscious connection, not conquest or a mere transaction. This chapter is your essential guide to liberating your sexuality from the shackles of performance anxiety and restrictive societal expectations. It's about moving towards genuine, respectful, and deeply satisfying sexual exploration within an ethical framework.

Beyond Performance: Redefining "Good Sex"

For far too long, male sexuality has been framed as a performance, a checklist of achievements. We're bombarded with messages to "get off," to "satisfy" our partner (implying their orgasm is our responsibility), or to "conquer" sexually. This mindset tragically leads to a focus on technique rather than presence, and can leave partners feeling used, unseen, or like a means to an end not to mention leaving us feeling unfulfilled and disconnected.

Real-World Scenario: A man named Mark has been conditioned by porn and locker-room talk. During sex, he's constantly thinking about whether he's "lasting long enough" or performing a move correctly. He misses his partner's subtle signs of pleasure because his internal dialogue is dominated by a performance checklist.

In ethical nonmonogamy, the quality of each sexual encounter becomes paramount. It's no longer about collecting notches on a belt; it's about creating meaningful, truly consensual, and mutually fulfilling experiences. This demands a profound shift in focus: from "doing" to "being," from "taking" to "sharing," and from a transactional mindset to a relational one.

The Core Principles of Ethical Sexual Exploration

Embracing ethical sex means consciously integrating the principles of radical honesty, enthusiastic consent, and proactive care into your sexual interactions. These aren't abstract concepts; they are the bedrock of truly liberating and respectful sexual encounters.

Prioritizing Enthusiastic and Ongoing Consent

Consent is not a one-time "yes." It's an ongoing conversation, a dynamic process of continuously checking in and ensuring active willingness from all parties.

Verbal Affirmation: Make asking for consent a natural and pleasurable part of your interactions. Questions like, "Does this feel good?" or "Are you comfortable with this?" enhance intimacy, rather than disrupting it. These also help you learn your partner and become a better lover for them resulting in you being a better lover for, YOU.

Reading Body Language (and Its Limits): While verbal consent is primary, pay attention to non-verbal cues. If you detect any hesitation, discomfort, or silence— STOP IMMEDIATELY and verbally clarify. Never assume.

The "FRIES" Acronym: Remember that consent must be Freely Given, Reversible, Informed, Enthusiastic, and Specific. Any "maybe" or a lack of an explicit "yes" means you stop, clarify, and respect the boundary.

Application: The next time you're intimate, pause mid-encounter and ask, "How are you feeling? Is this still good for you?" Pay attention to their response, both verbal and non-verbal, and adjust accordingly.

Mutual Pleasure: The Shared Journey

Ethical sex focuses on everyone's pleasure and well-being. It's a collaborative dance where both (or all) parties are active participants in creating enjoyment.

Communicate Desires Openly: Share what you like, what your fantasies are, and what you're curious about. Once again, this communication helps you create a sexual world that is truly molded just for you and your partner. Explore, discuss, and have fun doing it. Don't be afraid to let your "Freak Flag Fly". This invites your partner into your world and makes them an active collaborator. This level of communication also helps to build an even deeper trust in each other and a stronger bond.

Ask About Their Pleasure: Make their experience as important as your own. Ask, "What feels best for you right now?" or "How can I make this more pleasurable for you?" Don't be afraid to ask them questions. Just as before, talk during foreplay and sex. Learn about each other and what you like and don't like. This will take your sexual experiences from "run of the mill fun" to truly "orgasmic".

Focus Beyond Orgasm: While orgasm is great, it should never be the only goal. Explore sensuality, different forms of touch, and prolonged pleasure. Sometimes the most profound pleasure comes from shared vulnerability and deep presence rather than just a quick climax.

Real-World Scenario: Emma and Alex, a non-monogamous couple, decided to explore sensuality beyond traditional sex. They spent an evening using feathers and massage oils with no goal of orgasm. Their connection deepened as they realized that pleasure wasn't just about release, but about the journey of shared sensation.

Shame-Free Exploration: Embracing Your Desires

The pervasive societal conditioning around male sexuality often creates deep-seated shame around natural desires. Ethical sex requires actively shedding this internalized shame.

Internal Acceptance: Understand that your desires (as long as they are consensual and ethical) are not "bad" or "dirty." They are a natural, vibrant part of who you are. Stop letting societal norms or what's "socially acceptable" as the guide for what should and shouldn't "turn you on". Yes, there are some things that are ethically and morally unacceptable and by no means am I saying they are ok. You can get into whatever kinky, wild **shit** you want, but the line is clear: **no lasting damage to anyone**—especially not to your own damn mental state. Keep it safe, keep it consensual, and get yours.

Openness with Partners: Be willing to discuss your kinks, fantasies, and curiosities with potential partners. This creates a space for genuine connection and ensures alignment of sexual interests and boundaries.

Boundaries of Comfort: While exploring, it's crucial to respect your own comfort zones. Just because you're curious about something doesn't mean you have to do it, or that your partner has to agree.

Safe Sex Practices: Responsibility in Action

In nonmonogamy, safe sex is not just about personal health; it's a fundamental ethical responsibility to all partners in your network. It's a cornerstone of care and respect.

Open Dialogue: Make discussions about STI status, testing frequency, and preferred barrier methods a standard, non-negotiable part of every new sexual connection. This is not awkward; it's mature and caring.

Consistent Use: Use barrier methods (condoms, dental dams, etc.) consistently and correctly, unless all partners in a defined connection have explicitly discussed and consented to other arrangements.

Get Tested Regularly: Lead by example. Knowing your own status and getting tested regularly (e.g., every 3-6 months) protects both yourself and all your partners.

Real-World Scenario:

Sam, a man who practices ethical nonmonogamy, gets tested for STIs every three months and always uses condoms with new partners. He openly discusses his sexual health with all his partners and encourages them to do the same. This level of care not only protects everyone but also builds immense trust.

The Noble Lover: A Journey of Discovery

The outdated "conquest" mindset views sex as a battle to be won. The ethical "connection" mindset, however, sees every sexual encounter as a rich opportunity for shared vulnerability and intimacy.

Presence Over Performance: Consciously shift your focus from external validation to being fully present in the moment. Pay attention to your partner's responses and the shared experience unfolding between you.

Aftercare is Essential: Aftercare deepens intimacy and reinforces care. The conversation doesn't end when the clothes come back on. Offer physical comfort and check in: "How are you feeling now, physically and emotionally, after our time together?"

Integrity in Casual Sex: Even if an encounter is purely casual, it still demands the highest level of ethical behavior. Be transparent about your intentions and prioritize the other person's comfort and pleasure.

Embracing ethical sex is a continuous journey of self-discovery, relational growth, and profound liberation. When you approach sex with unwavering presence, enthusiastic consent, genuine care, and a profound desire for mutual joy, you don't just become a good lover; you become a truly noble one. This path ensures that your sexual freedom amplifies connection and well-being, rather than causing harm.

Chapter 6
Relationship Styles That Work for Men Crafting Your Authentic Connections

Remember that friend who tried to force himself into a monogamous mold, even though he deep down knew it wasn't truly him? He likely ended up miserable, feeling constrained, and possibly causing unintentional hurt by not being authentic. The liberating news is: you don't have to do that.

You are not obligated to squeeze yourself into a predefined relationship box. The fundamental key to navigating this landscape with integrity is **clarity**: What are you genuinely looking for, and are you being relentlessly honest about it with yourself and others?

This chapter will guide you through understanding, choosing, and most importantly, communicating your preferred relationship style. By understanding the various ethical non-monogamous (ENM) structures, you can find a model that truly resonates with your authentic desires and lifestyle. This self-awareness, combined with transparent communication, is crucial for building fulfilling connections that honor everyone involved and avoid unnecessary heartache.

Relationship Shorthand: Finding Your Fit

While it's important not to get hung up on rigid definitions, having a basic understanding of common ENM terms can be incredibly helpful. Think of them not as restrictive cages, but rather as useful signposts on a complex map.

Monogamish: A relationship that is primarily monogamous but allows for specific, agreed-upon exceptions for sexual encounters with others. It's traditional monogamy with intentionally flexible boundaries. This type of relationship could be a couple who are "swingers". It just means you get to scratch an itch, but **only** where you and your partner set specific boundaries. We could get into all the crazy intricacies and dynamics, but that fun is for another book entirely.

Open Relationship: The main gig, also known as the main relationship, is still the main gig, but you're both free to go get some from other people. You and your partner have to draw up the rulebook—specifically on how much emotion you're allowed to feel for the outside partners if any is allowed at all. Clearly defined boundaries and open communication are key in this dynamic.

Polyamory: This isn't just about screwing around or having a side piece; it's about building multiple serious, legitimate relationships at the same time. The core rule is full transparency and consent—everyone knows the deal, and you're investing in multiple deep connections. These are triads, quads, and even higher numbers. This is a very difficult dynamic and just as before communication and honesty are absolute key to making lifestyles such as this work.

Solo Polyamory (Solo Poly): You're playing the poly game, but you're the only CEO of your life. You have multiple deep partners, but you refuse to merge lives, finances, or move in with anyone. Your autonomy is the mission; no one gets to move up the traditional "relationship escalator."

Relationship Anarchy (RA): Throw out the rulebook and all the labels. You treat every connection—from a hookup to your best friend—with the same respect, making rules for each bond individually. No relationship is automatically "more important" just because it's labeled "romantic." It's all custom-built.

Casual Dating/Friends with Benefits (FwB): It's **strictly physical.** The whole point is to **get off with no strings attached.** You both have a clear, mutual understanding that there is **zero expectation** of a serious, long-term romantic relationship. Period.

Step 1: Self-Reflection Before the Conversation

Before you can effectively communicate your relationship style to others, you need to be crystal clear with yourself. This involves a courageous process of honest self-interrogation and deep introspection. Don't skip this step; it's foundational.

What genuinely excites me? Be honest about your primary drivers. Is it deep, multifaceted love with multiple people, or is it primarily the freedom to have diverse sexual experiences?

What are my limits? What am I realistically capable of offering in terms of time, emotional bandwidth, and energy? Over-promising leads to burnout and hurt. If you work 60 hours a week, you might only have the capacity for one deep connection and a few very casual ones, not a complex polycule.

What are my fears? Am I seeking non-monogamy to genuinely expand love, or am I running from commitment or a fear of being alone? Acknowledge these fears, as they will inevitably surface.

What kind of lifestyle do I want? Does a busy travel schedule or a desire for a minimalist life make independent dating more realistic than building a complex, interwoven polycule? Consider how your relationship choices integrate with your broader life goals.

Personal "Relationship Menu": Consider outlining what you can genuinely offer and what you are genuinely looking for in different types of relationships. This personal "menu" serves as an internal compass, helping you clarify your needs and communicate them effectively.

Example: "I can offer one deep, long-term, nesting partnership with shared finances and daily communication. I can also offer one or two additional romantic, non-nesting connections with weekly dates and strong emotional intimacy. I am also open to casual sexual connections with minimal emotional obligation."

Step 2: Communicating Your Relationship Style

Once you have a clearer, more honest picture of what you're looking for, the next crucial step is to communicate it proactively and transparently.

Lead with Your Truth (Early and Often): Don't wait until someone is emotionally invested. Be upfront about your relationship philosophy when meeting new people. This respects their time and autonomy.

Dating App Profile Example: "Ethically non-monogamous and currently in a polyamorous relationship. I'm excited to meet kind, communicative people for romantic connections."

First Date Example: "Before we go further, I want to share something important about my relationship philosophy. I'm ethically non-monogamous, and I'm currently [describe your specific situation]. How do you feel about non-monogamy in general?"

Define Your Boundaries and Expectations Explicitly: Never assume your partner knows what a label like "open" or "polyamory" means to you. Be specific about your agreements, limitations, and desires.

Example: "For me, being 'open' means I can pursue casual sexual connections, and I'm comfortable with you doing the same. Our agreements include always using condoms with other partners and having at least two dedicated date nights for just us each week."

Listen to Understand (Don't Sell or Persuade): Your goal is not to convince someone. Your goal is to find genuine compatibility. Actively listen to their boundaries, fears, and concerns without judgment or defensiveness. Be prepared for a negotiation, not a monologue.

Be Prepared for "No": Not everyone is interested in ENM, and that is perfectly okay.

Respect their choice immediately and gracefully. A clear "no" now saves immeasurable pain and heartache later. The freedom in finding your authentic relational fit is immense. It allows you to build relationships that are founded on proactive consent, radical honesty, and profound mutual respect from the ground up. This is precisely where the Noble Slut truly blossoms—in relationships built on truth, shared understanding, and intentional design, rather than unspoken expectations or inherited scripts.

Chapter 7
Masculinity Reimagined: The Courage to Shed Armor

What if the "strongest" thing a man can do is precisely what he's been taught to avoid: shed his armor, reveal his authentic self, and embrace his full emotional spectrum?

For generations, the prevailing script for masculinity has been dangerously narrow, demanding dominance, the suppression of emotion, and a transactional approach to sexual conquest. It's time to fundamentally rewrite that script.

A new, evolved masculinity means having the courage to feel every emotion, from joy to fear, from tenderness to sadness. It's about embracing vulnerability not as a weakness, but as a profound source of strength and deeper connection. It means wielding power through influence and inspiration, not through coercion. It signifies cultivating sexual confidence without objectification, and forging brotherhood without bravado.

A real man in this new paradigm leads with presence, not performance. This chapter explores how consciously shedding outdated, harmful notions of masculinity can profoundly liberate you, transform your relationships, and positively impact the world around you.

The Crisis of Traditional Masculinity: A Cage of Expectations

For far too long, the prevailing definition of masculinity has served as an invisible, yet suffocating, cage for men. This outdated script has demanded adherence to a rigid set of traits that, while seemingly offering a sense of "power," ultimately lead to isolation, shallow relationships, and immense internal suffering. It has forced men to repress natural human emotions and instincts.

This traditional model has typically demanded:

Emotional Stoicism: The ingrained messages like "Man up" teach men to bottle up their feelings. This leads directly to higher rates of depression, anxiety, and an inability to connect deeply with themselves or others.

Aggression and Dominance: The idea that a "real man" must always be in charge. This fuels conflict, suppresses collaboration, and fundamentally damages respectful, egalitarian relationships.

Sexual Objectification: Women and other marginalized genders are reduced to their sexual utility. This leads to a profound lack of empathy and ultimately results in unsatisfying, superficial sexual encounters devoid of true intimacy.

Self-Reliance to a Fault: The deeply damaging belief that asking for help is a sign of weakness. This leads to profound isolation, unaddressed mental health issues, and quiet suffering.

Competitiveness and Hierarchy: Relationships with other men become about proving who's "alpha," rather than fostering genuine support and camaraderie. This toxic "bro culture" comes at the expense of authentic connection.

The Noble Slut fundamentally rejects this outdated, harmful script. He understands that true power comes from integration, not repression.

Pillars of the New Masculinity: Expanding Strength

Reimagining masculinity isn't about becoming "less of a man." It's about expanding your definition of strength to consciously include qualities traditionally deemed "soft," which are, in fact, incredibly powerful and essential for thriving in complex relationships. Masculinity, in this new light, is a continuous journey of growth, not a fixed state.

The Courage to Feel and Express Emotion

True strength lies not in suppressing emotions, but in the courage to acknowledge, process, and express them authentically. This is emotional mastery, not emotional absence.

Practice Emotional Literacy: Actively learn to identify and name your feelings beyond simplistic categories like "fine" or "angry." Use tools like an emotion wheel to expand your emotional vocabulary. The more accurately you can name a feeling, the more agency you gain over it.

Share Your Vulnerability (Appropriately): With trusted partners and close friends, practice expressing your fears, insecurities, and needs. This is the fastest, most effective way to build deeper, more authentic intimacy.

Process Emotion, Don't Project: When feeling something intense (like jealousy or anger), rather than instinctively lashing out, use the tools from Chapter 4

(Acknowledge, Self-Sooth, Curiosity) to process it internally. Understand its roots before you communicate your needs constructively.

Real-World Scenario: David, a software engineer, used to suppress his emotions. After a stressful project, he found himself snapping at his partner. Recognizing this pattern, he began journaling and sharing his feelings, saying, "I'm feeling really overwhelmed with work." This shift not only improved his relationship but also enhanced his professional performance as he became more self-aware and communicative.

Power Through Presence, Not Control

Genuine power emerges not from needing to control others, but from being fully present, deeply self-aware, and impactful in your interactions. This is about influence, respect, and trust.

Active Listening: As discussed in Chapter 3, being fully present when someone speaks—listening to truly understand, not just to formulate a reply—is an immense display of respect and strength.

Self-Regulation: The capacity to manage your own emotional state, impulses, and reactions, especially in challenging situations, shows immense inner strength. It prevents reactivity and destructive behavior.

Influence vs. Control: Instead of trying to control a partner's choices, focus on clearly communicating your own boundaries and needs. For example, a man embodying new masculinity doesn't forbid his partner from seeing someone new; he clearly states, "My boundary is that I need clear and transparent communication about your schedule."

Real-World Scenario: Alex, an entrepreneur, used to micro-manage his relationships, believing that control equated to power. By practicing active listening and self-regulation, he learned to trust his team and communicate his needs more effectively. This shift allowed him to lead with presence rather than performance, fostering a more harmonious work and personal life.

Sexual Confidence Without Objectification

Sexual confidence in the new masculinity is rooted in deep self-knowledge, profound respect for others' autonomy, and a genuine desire for mutual pleasure and connection.

See the Whole Person: Consciously recognize that your partner is a complex individual with rich thoughts and feelings. They are not merely a body for your gratification. This fundamental shift makes sexual interaction deeper and more respectful.

Prioritize Consent as a Continuous Dance: True sexual confidence means confidently asking for consent at every step and respecting boundaries without pushing. It's about building trust and safety through enthusiastic, ongoing consent.

Embrace Shared Pleasure: Understand that your pleasure is profoundly enhanced when you are genuinely invested in your partner's enjoyment and satisfaction. This is a collaborative, co-created art form, not a solo performance.

Self-Acceptance in Desire: Confidently embrace your own sexual desires and curiosities without shame, knowing that ethical expression and consensual exploration make them healthy aspects of your being.

Real-World Scenario: Sam, a graphic designer, used to view sexual encounters as conquests. After a conversation with a friend, he realized the importance of seeing his partners as whole individuals. He started practicing consent and mutual pleasure, saying, "I want to make sure you're comfortable and enjoying this as much as I am." This shift not only improved his sexual relationships but also deepened his emotional connections.

Brotherhood Rooted in Support, Not Bravado

Redefine your relationships with other men to be spaces of genuine connection, authentic vulnerability, and mutual upliftment, completely free from the competitive, judgmental, and homophobic undertones of traditional "bro culture." It's perfectly ok to be a "Man's Man" without treating every other man as if you're both trying to attract the same partner.

Seek Authentic Connection: Instead of bonding solely over conquests or bravado, seek out deeper connections based on shared values and vulnerabilities.

Offer and Accept Support: Break the cycle of self-reliance. Be willing to openly ask for help when you're struggling, and proactively offer genuine, non-judgmental support to other men.

Challenge Toxic Masculinity: Be willing to courageously call out sexist jokes, homophobic remarks, or belittling comments in your peer groups. Be an active part of the solution, not a silent bystander.

The Liberating Power of the New Masculinity

Embracing this reimagined masculinity is a deeply, profoundly liberating act. It frees you from the exhausting burden of constant performance, the crushing isolation of emotional repression, and the moral compromises inherent in objectification. It allows you to build stronger, more authentic, and more fulfilling relationships—not just with romantic partners, but with friends, family, and most crucially, with your own integrated self.

This is how the Noble Slut embodies true strength: not by dominating, controlling, or conquering, but by fearlessly connecting with integrity, profound compassion, and unwavering courage.

Provocative Insight: The Erotic Power of Vulnerability

In the realm of intimacy, vulnerability is often the most potent aphrodisiac. When a man can shed his armor and reveal his authentic self—his fears, his desires, his kinks, his dreams—he invites his partner into a space of profound trust and connection. This vulnerability can be deeply erotic, as it allows for a level of intimacy that transcends the physical. It shows a depth of character and courage that is rare and valuable. It's a reminder that true sexual confidence is not about conquest, but about the courage to be seen, fully and authentically.

Chapter 8
Being an Ally to Women, Queer Folks, and the Sex-Positive Community

Being a Noble Slut isn't just about what you do in bed. It's about how you show up in the world. Ethical men don't isolate their liberation—they integrate it. If your personal sexual freedom doesn't include making room for others to feel safe, seen, and supported, then what you're practicing isn't freedom. It's a privilege in disguise.

Being an **ally** isn't about getting applause for being "one of the good guys." It's about interrogating your conditioning, stretching your empathy, and standing the hell up— especially when it's inconvenient, uncomfortable, or confrontational.

Allyship means consciously making space for identities, desires, and stories that aren't yours. It means asking yourself: What am I doing with the power I have? Am I using it to include—or to ignore? If you're serious about being ethically non-monogamous and emotionally literate, then allyship isn't a bonus feature—it's the foundation.

The Freedom of Empathy

This journey is deeply personal, but no revolution worth having is just about you. **Freedom that only applies to you is just another form of domination.**

As a man—especially a cisgender, straight, or white man—you move through society with unearned advantages. You may not feel powerful, but the world is often structured in ways that assume your comfort, safety, and desires are the default. Allyship is how you flip that script.

This isn't about virtue signaling. It's about **empathy with teeth.** Allyship isn't passive compassion—it's active participation in the dismantling of systems that harm the people you say you care about.

The Muscle of Allyship: How to Show Up

Allyship is not a badge. It's a muscle that requires consistent flexing—especially when no one's watching.

Listen and Learn (Without Demanding to Be Fed)

The world already listens to men—your job now is to listen better. Your growth depends on hearing diverse voices on their terms.

Seek Out Diverse Voices: Read **"Pleasure Activism"** by Adrienne Maree Brown. Watch Alok Vaid-Menon speak about gender on Instagram. Sit with the discomfort and let it teach you something.

Stop Expecting Free Education: If someone shares their experience with you, it's a gift—not a Google substitute. If a queer friend mentions being misgendered at work, don't ask for a lesson on pronouns. Instead say, "I'm sorry that happened. Do you want to talk about it, or would you rather just hang out?" Then, go educate yourself.

Believe Survivors: Validate, don't minimize. When a woman says her date made her feel unsafe, don't play devil's advocate. Don't say, "He probably didn't mean it." Say: "That's awful. I believe you. What do you need right now?"

Your Challenge: When was the last time you sat

through someone else's pain without making it about your guilt?

Check Your Privilege (With Grit, Not Guilt)

Privilege doesn't make you bad. But denying it makes you lazy. It's not your fault, but it is your responsibility.

Recognize Your Blind Spots: You might assume everyone feels safe walking home after a party. The reality is that women and queer folks often risk harassment or assault. An easy adjustment? Offer to walk them to their car—not as a savior, but as an act of solidarity.

Respect Boundaries Like They're Sacred: When a partner says, "not tonight," that's not a puzzle to decode. It's a boundary to honor. If you frame boundaries as obstacles instead of invitations to trust, you're part of the problem.

Be Conscious in ENM Spaces: Men are often overrepresented in poly circles or on dating apps. Ask yourself: "Am I consuming attention, or contributing to balance?" Share the emotional labor. And sometimes, just shut up so others can shine.

Your Challenge: This week, offer support when someone opens up about harm—without centering yourself.

Speak Up and Intervene (Even When It Costs You)

Your silence serves the status quo. Your discomfort doesn't outweigh someone else's harm.

Call Out Harmful Behavior: When a friend jokes about "turning a lesbian straight," speak up. Say: "That's not even a joke, man—it's **creepy.** It tells women you see them as a conquest or a project, not a person. You want to be the guy who makes women feel unsafe?

Disrupt Misinformation Boldly: If someone says, "Non-monogamy is just cheating with permission," counter them. "Actually, it's the opposite. Ethical non-monogamy requires more honesty and communication than most monogamous relationships."

Promote Consent Culture: Advocate for **FRIES** consent (Freely given, Reversible, Informed, Enthusiastic, Specific) like your integrity depends on it. In a group setting, say, "Let's make sure everyone here is enthusiastically on board. No pressure, no guessing."

Your Challenge: When was the last time you made another man uncomfortable in the name of making the world safer?

Support Inclusive Spaces

Being "sex-positive" doesn't just mean being down for threesomes. It means supporting the spaces that make authentic expression possible for everyone. It's not our place to judge or shame someone's desires, kinks, etc. Don't yuck someone else's yum. It may not be your cup of tea, but a real man isn't a Karen and stays in his own lane supporting his fellow man as he walks to the beat of his own personal drum.

Amplify Voices from the Margins: Share that podcast by a disabled kink educator. Recommend a book by a non-binary polyamorist. Use your platform to redirect attention, not just reflect yourself.

Go Where You're Uncomfortable—Then Stay: Attend that panel on trans experiences in dating. Sit in a workshop on navigating race and kink. Don't just dip in for optics—show up with humility and stay long enough to transform.

Be Radically Welcoming: At a play party, notice a trans person standing alone? Say hello. Make eye contact. Offer warmth. Inclusion isn't just policy—it's practice.

Provocative Insight: If your version of sex-positivity only centers people who look and act like you, you're not a sex-positive man—you're a narcissist with lube.

The Ripple Effect: Redefining Manhood in Real Time

By committing to true allyship, you don't just make the world better for others—you evolve the very definition of manhood. You become the kind of man who doesn't just seek consent—you live it. You don't just preach respect—you model it.

You embody a masculinity that's expansive, emotionally literate, sexually liberated, and deeply accountable. That's rare. That's needed. That's revolutionary. The old masculinity dominated. The new masculinity co-creates. Your integrity in this work ripples outward: to your lovers, your friends, your community, your kids—hell, even strangers at the next consent workshop. You're not just the product of your culture anymore. **You're a man who rewrites it.**

Final Challenge: This week, pick one of the actions above and do it. Are you willing to be that man?

Chapter 9
The Slut Code – Your Unapologetic Manifesto

Welcome, brother.

You've made it this far, which means you're not like the others. You've wrestled with the toxic myths, stared down your inherited shame, and dared to question the old scripts. You didn't just peek behind the curtain—you tore it down. And now, standing in the wreckage of the lies that once defined masculinity, you are finally free to ask the most dangerous question of all:

"What kind of man do I actually want to be?"

This isn't just another chapter—it's your battle standard. A call to arms. Your unfuckwithable moral compass, forged not in compliance, but in courage. This is your Code—The Slut Code.

These aren't rules. Rules are for boys afraid of punishment. This is something far more dangerous: a sovereign man's oath. A code of erotic honor. A manifesto for the unapologetically free.

If you're looking for loopholes, shortcuts, or permission to manipulate your way into someone's pants— close the book now. This isn't for you. But if you're ready to walk the razor's edge of radical self-responsibility, brutal honesty, and sacred sexuality—then brother, this is your inheritance.

This is how the Noble Slut walks through the world—with his

head high, his pants zipped or unzipped with integrity, and his heart wide open.

Let's begin.

Why a "Code" and Not "Rules"?

Rules exist to corral sheep. They're externally enforced. They beg for permission, fear punishment, and breed cowards who play nice until no one's watching. Rules as they say are meant to be broken.

A "**Code**", however, is internal. A code lives in your bones and is the steel in your spine. It doesn't ask for compliance; it demands alignment. It doesn't whisper "don't get caught"; it roars **"be the man who doesn't need to hide." A Code is challenge to yourself and is the ruthless truth of who you are.**

The Slut Code doesn't give a damn if you're liked. It demands you be **real, straight, and unbound.** This isn't a safety net; it's a **crucible.** It will challenge your every move, call out your **bullshit**, and **smash your ego** if you need it. But once the weak part of you is in the rubble, you will finally stand up as the **man you were always meant to be.**

That transformation—that self-mastery—that guide for life is bound and governed by one simple thing:

The Slut Code.

The Slut Code: 6 Tenets of the Unapologetically Noble Man

Don't Lie to Get Laid. Ever.

Let's rip the band-aid: Lying to sleep with someone isn't "game"—it's an assault on their consent. Every omission, every evasion, every "let's not get into that tonight" is a coward's way to rob someone of their educated choice. It's manipulative and duplicitous.

If you can't be fully seen, you don't deserve to be touched.

The Real Game is This: Be so honest, so undeniably transparent, that you magnetize the ones who crave exactly who you are.

Own your truth before you unzip your pants. Otherwise, keep them on.

Know Your Intentions, Speak Them Without Flinching.

If you don't know what you want, you're a loaded gun with no target—dangerous to everyone, including yourself.

Be honest: Are you here to fuck? To connect? To explore? Whatever it is—own it.

Stop using ambiguity as a tool. Ambiguity is emotional fraud. It's a coward's way of getting their cake and ghosting it, too.

Before the date: Ask yourself, "What do I actually want from this?" Then say it. Out loud. With spine.

Be Safe. Be Kind. Be about these Relentlessly.

There's nothing sexy about recklessness.

Physical safety: Get tested. Talk about your STI status. Use protection unless you've explicitly agreed not to. Respect every single boundary like it's sacred.

Emotional safety: No ghosting. No stringing along. No vague exits, hoping they "get the message." Speak with care. Leave with clarity and honesty. Always maintain your integrity.

You are not just another body. You are a walking nervous system with a ripple effect. So is every person you touch. Act like it.

If You Fuck Up, Own It. Fully.

You're not perfect. But you can be powerful. And true power comes from owning your shit without flinching. No blame-shifting. No gaslighting. No "sorry if you felt" cowardice. Just this: **"I did this. It hurt you. I see that. I'm sorry. What can I do to repair?"**

That's how trust is rebuilt. That's how kings operate. Let your mistakes make you mightier— not smaller.

Treat Every Lover Like a Human Being—Not a Fucking Trophy

We've been conditioned to collect women like high scores. Stories for the locker room. Notches on a headboard.

That's not noble. That's narcissistic masturbation dressed up as manhood. Every person you share intimacy with is not a prop in your origin story—they are a sovereign, sentient being with their own desires, fears, and boundaries.

Respect them like you respect your own freedom.

The way you talk about others reveals your true character when the lights go off.

Leave People Better Than You Found Them

This isn't just about dating—it's about legacy.

Leave fingerprints of integrity, presence, and power on everyone you encounter.

- Did your words make them feel seen?

- Did your presence make them feel safe?

- Did your honesty give them clarity? Whether it's a one-night stand or a lifelong partner, your impact should echo long after your touch has faded.

Tools for Living the Code: This code isn't just a set of ideas; it's a way of life. Here are some tools to help you live it out loud, unapologetically, and with deep fucking honor.

The Wallet Card / Pocket Code

Print this out, fold it up, and keep it in your wallet. When you're feeling lost or need a gut check, a quick glance will bring you back to your true north.

THE SLUT CODE
6 Tenets of the Unapologaictely Noble Man

• Don't Lie to Get Laid, Ever

• Know Your Intentions,
Speak Them Without Fliching

• Be Safe Be Kind

• If You Fuck Up, Own It Fully

• Treat Every Lover
Like a Human Being

• Leave People Better
Than You Found Them

THE SLUT CODE

I live with erotic integrity
I speak my truth
I love without shame
I honor all bodies I touch
I am a Noble Slut, This is my Code

The Noble Slut Manifesto

This is your battle standard, a powerful declaration of your values. It's perfect for a framed print, a screensaver, or sharing with your community.

I am a man of desire—but not desperation. I seek connection—but not conquest.

I fuck with fire—but I lead with heart.

I do not hide. I do not manipulate. I do not ghost. I speak my truth, even when it terrifies me.

I honor everybody I touch as sacred.

I own my mistakes. I repair what I break. I leave people better than I found them. I walk the world with erotic integrity.

I am not ashamed. I am not confused. I am not lost. I am a Noble Slut.

This is my Code.

And I will live it—loudly, unapologetically, and with deep fucking honor.

The Brotherhood Agreement / Slut Pact

For men's circles, communities, or 1-on-1 mentorship, this agreement is a powerful way to hold each other accountable.

The Noble Slut Brotherhood Agreement

We, the undersigned, pledge the following:

I will never lie to obtain sex.

I will know and speak my intentions without manipulation.

I will create physical and emotional safety in every connection.

I will treat all lovers with dignity, never as trophies.

I will take full ownership when I fuck up—no dodging, no deflecting.

I will leave every soul I meet more empowered than before.

I will hold my brothers accountable to this Code—with love and fire.

"May our masculinity be fierce, not fragile. May our sexuality be sacred, not secretive. May our brotherhood be forged in truth, not silence."

Signed,

Name: _________________________ Date: ________

This Is Not the End—This Is the Emergence

You're not just a man now—you're a movement.

The Noble Slut isn't a gimmick. It's not a costume you wear to parties or a line you drop in bed.

It's a lifestyle. A personal revolution. A reclamation of what masculinity could be if it were built on clarity, compassion, and wild, unapologetic truth.

So, what now? You live it. You fall. You get up.

You speak your truth, even when your voice trembles. You lead.

You fuck with fire and leave no ashes.

And one day, someone will ask, "How the hell did you become a man like that?"

And you'll smile and say, "I stopped apologizing for my desires. And I started living by a code."

The world doesn't need more "good guys. It needs more…

"Noble Sluts."

Go, be the storm, the presence in the room that shifts the air. The man whose freedom is bought with honesty and integrity. The lover whose touch is safe, wild, and unforgettable.

This is your new beginning.

What bold, honest, terrifyingly beautiful step will you take today?

Epilogue
The Unwritten Chapter

You've turned the final page, but our conversation isn't over. This book wasn't meant to be a destination; it's a launchpad. The Slut Code is more than ink on a page—it's a living document, a compass for a journey that begins the moment you close this book.

The world will try to pull you back. It will whisper the old myths of what a man "should" be. It will tempt you with the easy, transactional comforts of the past. But you know better now. You know the true, expansive, and terrifyingly beautiful power that comes from living with integrity.

Your epilogue isn't on these pages. It's in the quiet courage of a new conversation, the brave vulnerability of a difficult apology, and the fierce honesty of a boundary set with love. It's in every conscious choice you make to honor yourself and others.

So, go. Write your own story. Be the man who doesn't just read about integrity—he lives it, breathes it, and bleeds it into every encounter. The world is waiting for you to begin.

Embrace your authentic self, honor your code, and be.... Noble.